P9-BAW-546

COUNTY OF BRANT
PUBLIC LIBRARY

Look for these

ROTTEN SCHOOL
books, too!

ROTTEN SCHOOL

GROWL LEARNING PIZZA!

GOT CAKE?

R.L. STINE

Illustrations by Trip Park

HarperCollins*Publishers*

A Parachute Press Book

For Sumner
–TP

Got Cake?
Copyright © 2007 by Parachute Publishing, L.L.C.
Cover copyright © 2007 by Parachute Publishing, L.L.C.

All rights reserved.
No part of this book may be used or reproduced in any manner whatsoever without written permission except in the case of brief quotations embodied in critical articles and reviews. Printed in the United States of America.

For information address HarperCollins Children's Books, a division of HarperCollins Publishers, 1350 Avenue of the Americas, New York, NY 10019.
www.harpercollinschildrens.com

Library of Congress Cataloging-in-Publication Data
Stine, R. L.
  Got cake? / R.L. Stine ; illustrations by Trip Park. — 1st ed.
    p. cm. — (Rotten School)
  "A Parachute Press book."
  Summary: In order to be named "Most Popular Rotten Egg" in the school yearbook, fourth-grader Bernie Bridges must figure out a way to prove that he is the most popular student at Rotten School.
  ISBN 978-0-06-123269-5 (trade bdg.) — ISBN 978-0-06-123270-1 (lib. bdg.)
  [1. Popularity—Fiction. 2. Boarding schools—Fiction. 3. Schools—Fiction.] I. Park, Trip, ill. II. Title.
PZ7.S86037Got 2007   2007002984
[Fic]—dc22   CIP
                                                              AC

Cover and interior design by mjcdesign
1 2 3 4 5 6 7 8 9 10
❖
First Edition

CONTENTS

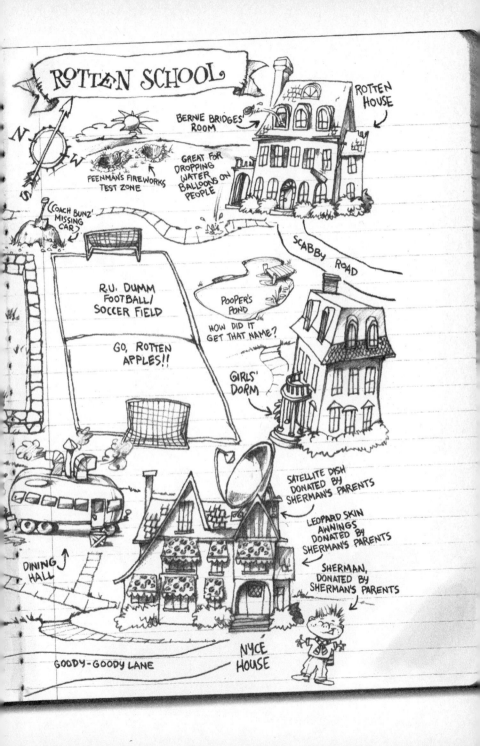

MORNING ANNOUNCEMENTS

Good morning, students. This is Headmaster Upchuck wishing you all a Rotten Day in every way. I know you are all proud to be Rotten Students. And I know you are looking forward to my morning tradition of reading the day's announcements.

SHUT UP! SHUT YOUR YAPS!

Sorry. I didn't mean to shout. You know I care deeply about you all.

SO SHUT UP AND LISTEN!

→ Coach Manley Bunz has a reminder for the first-grade track team. You'll win a lot more races if you all remember to run in the same direction.

Are you interested in water sports? Fourth-grade comedian Hardy Harhar will be demonstrating how to do a water spit at the second-floor water fountain at three today.

The after-school meeting of the fifth-grade Pick-Your-Nose-and-Eat-It Club will not be held today because THERE IS NO SUCH CLUB!

One of our oldest school traditions—the Tap-Dance-Swim-with-Arthropods Night—has been canceled because no one can remember what you're supposed to do.

Tonight is Lucky Dessert Night in the Dining Hall. It's called Lucky Dessert Night because Chef Baloney promises you won't heave your dinner until *after* dessert.

Chapter 1

HOW TO BE POPULAR

The most popular kid at Rotten School? Well, that's me, of course. Bernie Bridges. I suppose I'm probably the most popular fourth grader in history.

But don't ask me. Ask my *hundreds* of friends.

I'm a modest guy. I would never brag about how popular I am. Bragging is totally uncool.

How could I be the greatest dude who ever walked across campus if I bragged all the time?

So I'm not bragging. You can ask my twenty *best* friends.

They'd do *anything* for me. Anything.

It's easy to be surrounded by friends all the time. Really. You can do it, too. Here are my three rules for being popular:

1. Be generous
2. Be kind
3. Don't bite

I always try to follow all three rules.

That's why it was such a total shock to me when I had to *prove* how popular I am.

Whoa. Bernie Bridges in a popularity contest?

Could I lose? I don't *think* so.

I decided to prove it by throwing the biggest birthday party in the history of the known universe. But believe me, dudes and dudettes—it *wasn't* a piece of cake.

It all started on a sunny afternoon after classes. My friends and I were out on the Great Lawn, stomping on each other's shoes as hard as we could....

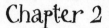

Chapter 2

NO PAIN, NO GAIN

STOMP.

"OWWWWWW!"

"YOWWWWWWWW!"

"Ohhhhh! It hurts! It HURTS!"

Maybe The Stomp hasn't come to your school yet. It will. It's the most popular sport at Rotten School now. Even more popular than opening your mouth wide at lunch and showing off your chewed-up glob of spinach.

You can see kids stomping on each other all over campus. And you can hear their cries of pain and watch them hopping up and down on one foot until the pain fades away.

"OWWWWW!"

"Give me a break!"

"YAAAAAIIIII!"

"Stop! You broke all my toes!"

The Stomp started whenever some dude would show up wearing new shoes or new sneakers. As soon as we saw the shiny, clean shoes, we'd all hurry to stomp on them and scuff them and smash them and make them look old.

It's just the natural thing to do when you see new shoes. It probably started with the cavemen.

We *begged* our parents not to send us new shoes.

We all knew how painful new shoes would be.

And then some guys got the idea to stomp on shoes that *weren't* new! That's how the sport was born. Some kid walks by. You stop him. You stomp your heel down on his shoe. Then you take out a stopwatch and see how long he can hop on one foot.

"OWWWW!

It hurts! It HURTS!"

Hop hop hop hop.

"Good work, Feenman!" I called to my friend. "You beat your old record. You hopped for twenty-three seconds."

I raised my stopwatch. "Try again, dude. If we can get it up to twenty-*eight* seconds, you can beat Joe Sweety's school record."

"But I don't *want* to beat the school record!" Feenman moaned. His face was bright red, and tears rolled down his cheeks. He stood on one leg and rubbed his sore foot.

8

"Don't be selfish," I said. "You know I bet Sweety twenty dollars we could beat his record."

I signaled to Crench, my other good buddy. "Get Feenman started."

STOMMMMMMP!

Crench tromped down on Feenman's shoe.

Feenman let out a howl and started hopping up and down on one foot.

"Go! Go! Go!"

I cheered him on as I stared at the stopwatch. That's another reason I'm popular. I'm always eager to cheer my guys on.

"Go! Go! Go!"

Feenman fell on his face after only fifteen seconds.

He lay in the grass, whimpering softly.

I could see he needed more cheering.

"One more try!" I shouted. "You can do it. You know my motto, Feenman. *No pain, no gain.*"

"But, Bernie—" he moaned. "*You're* not the one who's in pain!"

"But I'm the one who wants to *gain*," I said. "I'll gain twenty bucks if we beat Joe Sweety's record."

I motioned to Crench. "Get him on his feet. We're not quitters—are we?"

Crench bent down and started to pull Feenman up. My friend Nosebleed came by. He had a fat wad of tissues pressed to his nose.

"What's up?" I asked.

"Mmmmww, mwwwww," he said.

"I can't understand you," I said.

"That's cuz I have a fat wad of tissues pressed to my nose," he replied. "Wes Updood stomped on my new sneakers, and it gave me a nosebleed."

He shook his head sadly. "It ruined my yearbook photo. Do you believe I have a nosebleed in my yearbook photo? How totally uncool is that?"

Feenman

Gassy

April-May

Farley Mopes

Nosebleed

Sherman

Flora Peevish

Fauna Peevish

Joe Sweety

I slapped my forehead. "It's yearbook photo week? Oh, wow. I forgot all about it!"

"They call you when it's your turn," Crench said.

"I have to talk to them first," I said. "You *know* my photo has to be *perfect*. Kids won't buy the yearbook unless they know they're getting a perfect Bernie Bridges photo. Something to remember me by."

I spun away from them and starting jogging across the grass. The yearbook office was in the School House building, and I had to get there fast.

"Bernie—" I heard Crench shout. "Should I stomp on Feenman's foot and get him going again?"

"Stomp on your *own* foot!" I shouted back. "Maybe *you* can beat the record!"

"Okay. I'll give it a try.

OWWWWWWWWW!"

Chapter 3

Lighting Up the Dimples

The School House is a tall, redbrick building at the end of the Great Lawn. We call it Mouse House.

If we get bored in class, we count the mice that run by. Except some of us can't count that high.

We all sit with our legs crossed under us in class. That keeps the mice from climbing up your leg. Most of the time.

My friend Beast likes to play with the mice. He swings them by their tails and sends them sailing to the wastebasket near Mrs. Heinie's desk.

CLANNNNG!

"Yeaaaa! Three points!" Beast shouts every time he makes a basket.

Mrs. Heinie begs him to stop. But Beast just flashes her his special grin with the big white gobs of drool running down his chin.

And then, a few seconds later...

CLANNNNG!

"Yeaaaaa! Three points!"

I hurried down the empty hall and stopped at a door at the end. I read the words on the window: ROTTEN EGG.

That's the name of our school yearbook. The *Rotten Egg*. How did it get that name? Who knows? Maybe they just couldn't think of a better one.

I pushed open the door and looked around for the editor. He's a tall, skinny, redheaded sixth grader named Leif Blower.

Blower is really into the yearbook. He has a tiny silver egg stuck through one earlobe. And he wears a green-and-yellow cap that says: ASK ME ABOUT ROTTEN EGGS.

He always has a camera around his neck. Even in the shower. He says you never know when a good yearbook photo will come up.

"Yo—Blower!" I called. I didn't see anyone in the room.

"Yo, Blower! What's up?" I knew he had to be there. He never went to class. He just stayed in the *Rotten Egg* office all day and worked on the yearbook.

"Yo—Blower?"

Finally I spotted him on a tall stool against a wall. He had his face buried in a stack of photos on the table in front of him.

He kept shaking his head. "I can't decide," he said. "Bernie, maybe you can help me."

I hurried across the room. "What's the problem?"

He held up three photos. I squinted at them. I saw a window with gray curtains.

"Which photo of Headmaster Upchuck do you like best?" Blower asked.

I squinted at them again. "I don't see Headmaster Upchuck," I said. "I just see a window."

He frowned. "That's the problem. Upchuck is too short. His head didn't come up to the camera lens. I only got the window behind his desk."

"Maybe you should have lowered the camera a little," I said.

Blower scratched his head. "Maybe."

I took the photos from his hands and set them down on the table. "Can we talk?" I said. "I know you've been thinking about my yearbook photo. I'm here to help."

He scratched his head some more. "Maybe I can get Upchuck to stand on his desk," he said. "Or maybe I should get down on my knees to shoot him. I don't want to insult the little shrimp."

"About my photo," I said. "I'd like a blue sky in the background. With just a few puffy clouds. Think you can handle that?"

Blower didn't answer. He stared blankly at me.

"I need backlighting," I said. "You know. To capture the silky glow of my hair. I'm not sure which is my best side. You'll have to shoot me from both sides. Then we can decide later—okay?"

He still stared at me blankly.

"Or maybe we should do a straight face shot," I said. "I mean, we need to show off *both* of my dimples. Everyone says I have *killer* dimples. Shall we work out special lighting for that? Perhaps a light for each dimple?"

He blinked several times. "Sorry, Bernie," he said. "I didn't hear a word you said."

"But my photo—" I started.

He put a hand on my shoulder. "I've got something much more important to think about, Bernie."

More important than my yearbook picture?

What could that *be*?

Chapter 4

"ACK. ACK. ACK."

Blower picked up a bottle from the table and took a long drink from it. He made a face. "This root beer tastes funny."

"It isn't root beer," I told him. I took the bottle and read the label. "India Black Ink."

"ACK. ACK. ACK." Blower grabbed his throat and started hacking and coughing and sputtering.

"You should probably see the nurse," I said. "You're gonna scare people with that black tongue."

"ACK. ACK. ACK."

I picked up the root beer bottle—next to the

bottle of ink—and took a slurp. "But before you go," I said, "can we talk about my photo?"

"ACK. ACK. ACK."

He "*acked*" for another five or six minutes. Then he did some very loud spitting into a wastebasket.

Finally he sat down. "I think I'm back to normal," he said. His lips were black, and so were his teeth.

"Lookin' good," I said.

Why worry the poor guy?

"About my yearbook photo…" I started.

"Not now," Blower said, shaking his head. "I'm totally thinking about one thing. The Most Popular Rotten Egg."

I stared at him. "The *what?*"

"The yearbook is a hundred years old," he said. "Back then they had the Most Popular Rotten Egg page. They picked the most popular Rotten Student of the year, and the student was named Most Popular Rotten Egg. The student got a whole page in the yearbook all to himself. For the yearbook's hundredth birthday, we're bringing back the tradition."

"Wow! That's excellent!" I cried. I slapped Blower on the back. "This is so sudden. I didn't even know you were thinking of me. But I gladly accept. Shall we take the picture now?"

He stuck out his tongue. "Is my tongue black?"

"Maybe a little," I said. "I'm so excited about the Rotten Egg award."

"Bernie, I haven't decided who wins it," Blower said. "It's a big responsibility. I'm taking it very seriously."

"You won't be sorry," I said. "I'm too modest to say it, but everyone knows that Bernie B. is the most popular dude around here."

"I have to take my time and think hard about it," Blower said. "And I have to discuss it with Mr. Pupipantz, the yearbook adviser."

"I can pose tomorrow afternoon," I told him. "Let me get a haircut first. That'll give you time to talk it over."

Blower scratched his head. "I'm not so sure you're the winner, Bernie. After all, Sherman Oaks just gave me this video iPod with two hundred movies. That makes him *very* popular with me!"

I gasped. That spoiled rich kid Sherman Oaks was up to his old tricks.

"Blower," I said, "you wouldn't take a bribe—would you?"

He rolled the video iPod around in his hand. "Of course not," he said. "But I like that guy Sherman. He has a lot of class."

"But—but—" I sputtered.

"I'm keeping an open mind," Blower said. "Anyone who wants to be Most Popular Rotten Egg must *prove* that he or she is the most popular kid at school."

I squinted at him. "Prove it? How?"

Before Blower could answer, Mr. Pupipantz clomped into the room. He's a big, red-faced dude with a shiny bald head. He's shaped exactly like a bowling ball but a lot heavier. He always wears these tight sweaters that don't fit and show off about two inches of his hairy belly.

"Hi, Mr. Pupipantz," I said. I flashed him my best smile. "Leif and I were just talking about how popular I am."

Mr. Pupipantz shook a finger at me. "No tricks, Bridges," he barked. "No stunts. I'll be watching you to make sure you don't pull any tricks."

I gasped. "Huh? Me? Tricks?"

"Choosing Most Popular Rotten Egg is an important decision," Pupipantz said. "Give Leif and me a chance to make up our minds. We're going to be totally fair about this."

"Of course," I said. "But I—"

"By the way, Leif," Pupipantz interrupted. "Did that really nice guy Sherman Oaks leave one of those video iPods for me, too?"

Chapter 5

APRIL-MAY SAYS SOMETHING NICE

I really wanted to be Most Popular Rotten Egg. I knew I deserved it. Sherman Oaks was trying to buy it, the way he buys everything else. I couldn't let him get away with that. But how could I beat him?

Later that afternoon, I walked across the Great Lawn, thinking hard. In the distance I heard screams of pain and tearful sobs of guys getting their shoes stomped on.

Sure, it sounded like fun. But I wasn't interested.

I was thinking hard about popularity. I was thinking so hard, my eyes started to spin, my ears flapped

up and down, and my hair tried to fly right off my head.

"Whoa. Too hard. You're thinking *too* hard, Bernie," I told myself. I struggled to smooth my hair back down.

I can't help it. I'm a hard thinker.

I started thinking about having a birthday party. I'd invite everyone in school. Maybe kids from every school in the country. And I'd invite Blower. And he'd be wowed by how popular I am.

Everyone loves Bernie B. If only I could brag about it. But that's not like me.

Speaking of true love, up ahead on the path was *my* true love—April-May June. April-May is my girlfriend. She just doesn't know it yet.

Her blond ponytail wagged behind her, glowing under the afternoon sun. I could see her bright blue eyes, her warm smile.

I *know* she's nuts about me. But she's always so shy when I'm around. When she saw me coming, the shy thing started to run away.

"April-May—stop!" I shouted. "I want to ask you something!"

"The answer is,

she shouted back.

I love a girl with a sense of humor.

"April-May . . . gasp, gasp." I was panting hard by the time I caught up to her. "Answer one question. Who is more popular than me?"

She rolled her eyes. "Everyone," she said.

"Ha-ha! You're joking, right?" I said.

She rolled her eyes again. "I thought YOU were joking, Bernie," she said. "You're about as popular as what I just cleaned off the bottom of my shoe after walking near Pooper's Pond."

I laughed. "You love to tease me—don't you! That's how I know you like me."

She stuck a finger down her throat and made gagging sounds.

"Enough teasing," I said. "Come on. Make my day. Say something nice about me."

She gagged up her lunch. "Okay," she said finally. "Something nice." She thought hard. "Uh . . . Bernie, I think you're more popular than stomach flu."

A happy smile spread over my face. "See? I *knew* you could do it."

I turned and saw Leif Blower trotting over to us. "Yo—Blower. Whussup?" I called. "Lookin' good, dude!"

Blower gave April-May a big, black-toothed smile.

April-May's eyes twinkled when she saw him. She flashed him a bright smile and wrapped her arm around his. "Who's most popular?" she breathed into his ear. "I am—aren't I, Leify baby?"

He giggled. And blushed dark red. "Know what? I think maybe you are!" he said, nodding his head.

She squeezed his hand and rubbed her cheek against his. "I'm the most, most, most, most popular, aren't I?"

He giggled again. "Uh-huh" was all he could choke out.

I watched them walk off hand in hand.

"This is going to be more difficult than I thought!" I told myself.

I heard thundering foot-steps. The ground shook.

I spun around—and saw Jennifer Ecch. Stomping toward me, head lowered like an angry bull coming after a red flag.

Jennifer Ecch, the biggest, strongest, hulkiest girl at Rotten School. I call her Nightmare Girl.

But it doesn't matter what I call her. The Ecch is

totally in love with me.

But now as she thundered toward me, I froze in TERROR.

Because I could see the fierce gleam in her one brown eye and one blue eye.

And I knew what she planned to do.

She planned to do The Stomp on my foot!

Chapter 6

Why I Look Like a Duck

"Yowwwwwwwww!"

My scream sent leaves tumbling from the trees. I saw two birds fall out of the sky and land with two thuds on the grass.

I'll never forget the grin on Jennifer's face. When it came to The Stomp, she knew she *ruled*.

"Why are you screaming?" she cried. "That was a love tap."

A love tap?

My foot was buried *two feet* in the ground!

I tugged it out. My shoe looked like shredded wheat. I grabbed it with both hands and started hopping in agony.

CLICK, CLICK, CLICK.

I glanced up and saw Jennifer with a camera pressed to her face. She snapped picture after picture as I hopped on one foot.

"Look what you did!" I screamed. "My foot is totally FLAT! You gave me a webbed foot! I look like a DUCK!"

She laughed. "Keep hopping, Ducky Lips. I think you can set the school record."

"Don't call me Ducky Lips!" I screamed.

CLICK, CLICK, CLICK.

I couldn't hop anymore. My foot had swelled up to the size of a cantaloupe! I plopped down onto the grass. "What are you doing with that camera?" I cried.

CLICK, CLICK.

She plopped down beside me. She giggled and grabbed my arm.

"Ducky Lips, you crack me up," she said. Then she started planting wet, smoochy kisses up and down my arm.

She didn't stop until my arm was limp and soaked as a sponge.

Do you know how embarrassing it is to be in fourth grade and have a girl totally in love with you?

I sighed. "What about the camera?" I asked again.

"The shots of you hopping up and down are going to be *awesome* in the *Rotten Egg!*" she gushed.

"Excuse me?" I said.

She gave my shoulder a gentle slap—so gentle, it knocked me flat on the grass. "Ducky Whiskers, you *know* I'm the new photographer for the yearbook."

I stared at her until my glasses steamed up. "Huh? You? *You* work for the yearbook?"

She nodded.

I scooted away. She looked like she was going to give me another gentle tap.

"You're the Official Photographer for the *Rotten Egg?*" I asked.

She nodded again.

My mind whirred. I could feel my brain heating up inside my skull as I began to think. My ears started flapping again.

Now I couldn't lose! With Jennifer as *my* Official Photographer, *I couldn't lose!* (Maybe.)

Chapter 7

TOTAL EMBARRASSMENT

I jumped to my feet. I began to pace back and forth excitedly in front of Jennifer. "You know about the Most Popular Rotten Egg page?" I asked her.

She nodded. "Of course. I'm taking the photo of the winner."

She leaned forward and started pulling up clumps of grass from the ground with both hands. Then she stuffed them into her mouth and chewed on them.

I squinted down at her. "Why are you doing that?"

She shrugged. "MMMPH, MMMMPH. I like to keep busy."

I told you she's a beast.

"I want to win the Most Popular contest," I said.

A lopsided grin spread over her face. "You're already Most Popular with *me*, Honey Face." She grabbed my hand, jerked me back down to the ground, and began planting more smoochy kisses on my arm.

I had to shove her away when she started to chew the buttons off my shirt.

"Jen, listen to me," I begged. "You want to help me, don't you?"

She giggled. "Of course I'll help you. You're my wubby-wubby—aren't you?"

"Your WHAT?!" I screamed.

Her crooked grin spread all the way to her huge, floppy ears. "My wubby-wubby."

Oh, puke.

"Jennifer, please!" I begged. "Don't ever say that again. Please—*swear* you'll never say that again."

She giggled. "How do you want me to help you?"

"I want you to take a bunch of photos of me being popular," I said. "Follow me around with your camera. And whenever you see me being popular, snap a shot."

"Okay, Wubby-Wubby," she said.

"Please—no wubby-wubby!" I pleaded. "If you say it one more time, I'll have no choice. I'll have to leave school."

"So I take photos of everyone adoring you," Jennifer said. "Then what?"

"Then you snap a thousand photos of the huge crowd at my birthday party," I said. "Total proof of how popular I am."

She squinted at me with her one brown eye and one blue eye. "You're having a birthday party?"

"The biggest party in Rotten School history," I said. "Then you bring the stack of photos to Leif Blower. Blower will see that I'm the only choice. Piece of cake!"

Jennifer lumbered to her feet. "I'm late for hockey practice," she said. "Can I bake you a big birthday cake for your party? Please, please, please? Can I bake the cake?"

"Sure," I said. "The bigger the better."

She grinned. She had clumps of grass stuck in her teeth. "Thank you! Thank you! I'm going to bake the biggest birthday cake in history!"

She started to trot toward the hockey field. Then she suddenly turned and yelled at the top of her lungs: "Bye, Wubby-Wubby!"

I saw April-May and Leif across the grass. They HEARD her! They started to laugh. Other kids started laughing, too.

Oh, wow. I felt my face turn red. Laughter rang in my ears. I slumped to the ground. And I started pulling up clumps of grass and stuffing them into my mouth.

Hey—not bad!

Chapter 8

THE SECRET IS OUT

So far, the birthday party was just a brilliant idea. Now I had to get people working on it.

I knew I couldn't give the party for myself. How *lame* would that be?

Other kids had to throw the party for me.

You probably go home every day after school. But I can't. Rotten School is a boarding school. That means we all live at school.

My buddies and I live in a dorm called Rotten House. Actually, it's a run-down, beat-up old house with creaking floors, rattling windows, an inch of dust everywhere, and strange, furry bugs crawling up and down the walls.

We *love* it.

We can do whatever we want. No parents! And Mrs. Heinie, our dorm mother, is totally nearsighted. She can't see a thing we do.

How great is that?

I have a big room all to myself on the third floor. My friends Feenman, Crench, and Belzer are squeezed into the tiny room across the hall.

They don't mind. They know a popular guy like me needs plenty of room to practice being popular.

That night, I crossed the hall into Feenman, Crench, and Belzer's room. I stopped at the door—and gasped in surprise.

Crench's face and hair were gleaming bright red. He was standing totally still while Feenman slid a fat paintbrush up and down his jeans and T-shirt.

Painting him red.

I stepped into the room. Feenman's hobby is painting things red. He likes to paint kids' computer screens red when they're not looking. One night he sneaked into the School House and painted all the

windows in Mrs. Heinie's classroom red.

"Yo, Bernie," Feenman greeted me with a smile. "How does he look?"

"He looks red," I said. "Why are you doing this to him?"

"For Halloween," Feenman answered. "Cool, huh?"

"But—but—" I sputtered. "Feenman, Halloween is five months away!"

"No problem," he replied. "I used waterproof paint. No way it'll ever wash off."

Crench grinned at me through the thick, red globs of paint oozing down his head. "Scary, huh?"

"Scary," I said. "What are you supposed to be?"

"A dude who is red," he said.

I should have known.

Time to get the ball rolling. Time to put the party idea in their heads . . .

I dropped down onto the edge of their bunk bed. "You know, it's hard to keep a secret around here," I said.

Feenman bent down to paint Crench's sneakers. "Secret, Bernie?"

"Yeah. I heard your secret," I said. "I know you guys are planning a big surprise party for my birthday."

"We *are?*" they both replied.

Feenman carefully painted Crench's socks.

"Yeah, the secret got out," I said. "But listen, guys. Keep the party small, okay? I don't want kids to think I'm stuck-up. Just invite everyone in the whole school. And maybe a few hundred kids from other schools."

"No problem, Bernie," Feenman said.

"Yeah, no problem," Crench repeated. He scratched his head. Now his hand was smeared with red paint. "When did you say your birthday was?"

I laughed. "Don't tease me," I said. "I *know* you know the answer to that. I know you guys have been planning this party for weeks."

"Yeah. Right," Feenman said. He turned Crench around and started painting his butt red.

"Catch you later," I said. "Remember—make it a small party. Just invite everyone you can think of."

I stepped out into the hall, but I didn't go into my room. I pressed myself against the wall and eavesdropped on them.

"Did you know it was Bernie's birthday?" I heard Crench say.

"No," Feenman answered. "Think we should give him some kind of party?"

"I dunno," Crench replied. "Maybe."

Okay! I thought. *Well done, Bernie. That's a start.*

I tiptoed back to my room.

I'd put the idea into their heads.

I could already hear the whole school singing "Happy Birthday" to me.

Will that impress Leif Blower?

Does a duck swim backward in the spring?

Chapter 9

BELZER CAN'T KEEP A SECRET

I waited three days. Then I took Belzer aside in the Dining Hall during lunch.

Belzer must have eaten a big lunch. He couldn't button his school blazer. Underneath it he wore a red-and-white T-shirt. I pulled open the blazer and read the T-shirt:

I MAY BE STUPID BUT AT LEAST I'M UGLY.

I frowned at him. "Belzer, where do you get these loser T-shirts?"

He squinted at me. "You really think it's a loser shirt? My mother sent it to me."

49

Belzer grabbed a slice of pizza off the serving table. He tried to eat it whole but missed his mouth, and most of it went onto his shirt.

"Belzer, I know you and the guys are planning a big surprise party for me," I said. "It's going to be HUGE—right?"

He blinked. "Party?"

"Try to keep it small," I said. "I'm a modest guy. I'd like it to be small."

He picked a piece of pepperoni off his shirt and ate it. "Party? Bernie, I haven't heard anything about a party."

I laughed and slapped him on the back. "I see that little smile on your face, Belzer," I said. "You're so bad at keeping a secret!"

He blinked some more. "Party? Are you sure?"

I handed him another pizza slice. This time it went all over his forehead.

Did the guys forget about planning the party?

I decided they needed more reminding. So I called a Rotten House dorm meeting that night....

Chapter 10

I ♥ BERNIE

I herded everyone into the Rotten House Commons Room. That's like our living room, with comfy chairs and couches. Mrs. Heinie stood in the doorway, squinting at us through her thick glasses.

"You're looking really, really wonderful tonight, Mrs. H.," I said. "I love your new hair color—bright orange."

"It's not my hair. I'm wearing a shower cap," she said. "Hurry up and get this meeting over with, Bernie. I have to go upstairs and deworm my cat."

"No problem, Mrs. H."

I set a big carton down on a table and pulled out a few T-shirts. "Okay, dudes," I said. "Here are the official T-shirts for everyone to wear to my surprise birthday party. Do you like them better in blue or gray?"

I held up one of each. On the front they said: I ♥ BERNIE. And on the back they said: I ♥ BERNIE.

I wasn't taking any chances.

I reached into the carton. "And here are the party favors. Pictures of me, of course." I held them up. "Do you like this view or this view? I can't decide which is my best side. You get to vote since you're the ones who are throwing the party."

"Bernie, hold your horses," Mrs. Heinie said. She crossed the room and picked up a few T-shirts.

"I'd be honored for you to wear one, Mrs. H.," I said. "Let me see if I have your size. You take a small—right? No. Maybe a teeny-tiny."

She usually loves it when I do a little flattering. But she frowned and tossed the shirts down. "Bernie, what is this meeting about? You told me you wanted to discuss planting pansies and petunias around the statue of I. B. Rotten."

My mouth dropped open. "Pansies? Petunias? Mrs.

Heinie, how can you think about flowers? My friends here have been working so hard on my birthday party. I know they want to get it right. So I called this meeting to help them."

Her eyes goggled behind her glasses. "Party? What party? I'm the dorm mother. It's my job to know *everything* that's going on around here!"

"And you do it so well," I said. "You're an *awesome* snoop, Mrs. Heinie."

"Well," she said, "I haven't heard anything about a party."

I laughed. "You can't keep a secret. I see that smile on your face. You know about the party. I'll bet you've been helping the guys plan it, haven't you!"

Mrs. Heinie frowned. "But what about the pansies and petunias?"

"Yes, they would be nice for my party," I said. "But roses are my favorite. I know you're all planning to fill the room with roses—aren't you!"

Chapter 11

SHERMAN KNOWS HOW TO BE POPULAR

Was the party idea working?

Does a bear wear suspenders in the woods?

The answer was definitely *no*.

For the next few days I kept my eyes and ears open. But no one was talking about it. No one was making decorations or blowing up balloons. I searched every closet in Rotten House. No one had hidden away any birthday presents for me.

Friday afternoon, I saw Sherman Oaks with Leif Blower outside the Student Center. Sherman waved a hundred-dollar bill in front of Blower's face.

"Did you lose this?" he asked Blower. "I think I saw this crisp hundred-dollar bill fall out of your pocket." He stuffed the bribe money into Blower's blazer pocket.

Blower had a huge grin on his face. He touched knuckles with Sherman.

I clenched my fists so hard, my *knees* hurt! "I can't let Sherman Oaks bribe his way to Most Popular Rotten Egg," I told myself.

I knew my birthday party would win the day. But how could I get the guys to start planning it? Maybe I had to try a few other things first. Suddenly, I had an idea....

Chapter 12

BELZER IS A SPELLING CHAMP

That night, Belzer was in my room, sitting at my desk, doing my homework. He does my homework every night. Good kid, Belzer.

Tonight he was writing a history report for me. He looked up from the laptop. "Bernie, how do you spell FBI?" he asked.

"Well...spell it the best way you can," I said. "I've gotta talk to Feenman and Crench."

I heard noises from across the hall. Loud, cracking sounds.

I hurried into the guys' room. "Dudes—what's up?

What's that cracking noise?"

"We got tired of doing The Stomp," Crench said. "It hurt our feet too much. No one can walk."

"So we've all switched to knuckle cracking," Feenman said. He knotted his hands and cracked his knuckles really hard. I saw a bone poke through the skin on his middle finger.

That's *champion* knuckle cracking!

"No time for that, guys," I said. "We have to get busy. You have to help me."

CRAAAAACK.

Crench cracked his knuckles. Then his eyes bulged, and he let out a scream. "Oh, help! *Help* me!" He couldn't get his fingers untangled.

I had to get my pliers and pull them apart.

Crench retreated to his bunk and blew on his fingers.

"I do everything for you guys, right?" I said. "Everything. I'm always looking out for you. I even keep your money safe and sound for you. So now it's time for you to help *me*."

"What do we have to do, Big B?" Feenman asked. He was pushing the bone back into his finger.

"Just show up after class tomorrow," I said. "Get all the guys in the dorm. Meet me at the library after school."

Feenman and Crench stared at me. "Bernie," Crench said, "does our school have a *library?*"

"No one told us," Feenman said.

From my room across the hall I heard Belzer shout: "Bernie, how do you spell PTA?"

Chapter 13

SMILE FOR THE CAMERA

The next afternoon was crisp and cool. A strong wind kept blowing my balloons from side to side. And the party streamers fluttered noisily from the tree behind the library.

The guys from my dorm came bopping up, led by Feenman and Crench.

"Yo—dudes! Let's get this party started!" I shouted.

"Party?" Crench asked. "Huh? Is *this* your birthday party?"

"No. No way," I said. "This is my PRE-birthday party. It's the warm-up party. You know. To get everybody pumped for the *real* party."

They scratched their heads and stared at me.

"I've never been to a PRE-party," Belzer said. "What do we do?"

"No worries," I said. "What we do is, we *pretend* we're having a lot of fun." I clapped my hands. "Everybody start cheering. Come on, dudes—big smiles!"

I stuck out my arms. "Feenman! Crench! Pick me up!" I shouted. "Carry me around on your shoulders. It's my birthday—right? Parade me around. Let's hear it, guys. Everybody cheer for Bernie B.! Make it look real! Bring tears to my eyes!"

Feenman and Crench hoisted me onto their shoulders. I pumped my fists in the air. "Let's hear it for ME!" I yelled. "Everybody cheer now! Let's make this the best PRE-party ever. Everybody smile into the camera!"

Balancing on my friends' shoulders, I turned to Jennifer Ecch. "Are you ready?"

She nodded. "Yes, I'm ready. Only one problem."

"Problem?"

"I forgot my camera."

I let out a sigh and slid to the ground. My friends started walking away, grumbling.

"Don't anybody move!" I shouted. "Freeze! Everybody, freeze! This is a party—remember? Nobody leaves."

"Sorry, Honey Bunny," The Ecch said. "My camera is lost. I think I left it somewhere."

"Don't call me Honey Bunny," I said. "Don't worry about it. No problem!"

I turned to Belzer. "Run back to the dorm. Get my camera. It's on my dresser. Hurry. Some of the balloons are blowing away. And Beast is eating all the streamers!"

Belzer took off.

"It's cold out here," my friend Chipmunk complained. He was hugging himself and shivering. "Can't we go inside?"

"I have a nosebleed," Nosebleed whined.

"These streamers are making me thirsty!" Beast growled with a mouth full of crepe paper.

"Nobody move," I said. "This is gonna be a great PRE-party. You'll see."

They all booed and groaned and muttered mean,

nasty things under their breath.

Bad attitude.

You've probably figured out what was up. I wanted Jennifer to take a bunch of pictures of the guys cheering me and carrying me around on their shoulders. A big celebration with balloons and streamers.

She takes the pictures to Blower. And he says, "Wow. I guess these pictures are proof—Bernie *is* the most popular dude in school."

It *had* to convince him. We all know pictures don't lie—right?

A few minutes later Belzer came running back. Panting, he handed the camera to Jennifer.

"I'm ready, Honey Bunny," she said. She licked my face. Then she raised the camera to her brown eye.

"Okay. Take two!" I cried. "Feenman! Crench! Get me up on your shoulders. Let's go, everyone! Party time! Look happy! Let's hear the cheers. Pump your fists! Party! Party! Make it look real!"

The cheers went up. The guys all grinned and waved and clapped. Feenman and Crench paraded me back and forth as everyone went nuts.

Jennifer snapped shot after shot. She just kept clicking away.

We celebrated for at least twenty minutes. Jennifer took about a hundred shots.

Finally Feenman groaned. "Bernie, can I put you down? I've lost all feeling in my shoulder!"

"Me too!" Crench moaned. "My whole body is numb."

"Cut!" I shouted, sliding to the ground. "Cut! Good work, everyone! Great PRE-party! Awesome! Thanks for coming! See you at the *real* party, which I know you are busy planning!"

My friends all took off, heading back to the dorm. Beast stayed to pop the balloons with his two front teeth.

I turned to Jennifer. "Good work," I said. "Did you see those guys? Could there be any better proof of how popular I am?"

Jennifer rubbed her cheek against mine. "That's why you're my wubby-wubby," she whispered.

Yuck.

"Never mind that wubby-wubby stuff," I said.

"Get that film developed—fast. And take the shots to Blower."

Jennifer stared at the camera. "Film?"

"Yeah," I said. "Get it developed. I want Leif Blower to see it as soon as—"

"But—but—" Jennifer sputtered. "I thought your camera was a *digital* camera!"

"No *way*!" I said. "It's film."

I grabbed Belzer by the front of his shirt. "Did you put film in the camera? Tell me you put film in the camera."

He shook his head. "No, Big B. I can't tell you I put film in the camera…cuz I didn't."

I slapped my forehead. "Why not?"

"You didn't tell me to."

Jennifer opened the camera. We all stared inside. No film.

"My bad," Jennifer said. She grabbed my head with both hands and made a pouty face. "Bunny Breath, will you ever forgive me?"

"Jennifer, you're crushing my head into a raisin," I said.

"Oops. Don't know my own strength." She let go.

"What are we going to do now, Bunny Breath?"

"Don't panic," I said, trying to stretch my face back into shape. "Don't anybody panic. There's always Plan B!"

"Plan B?" Jennifer asked. "What's Plan B?"

"Well...Plan B," I said, "is thinking up what Plan B should be."

Chapter 14

BOOS
AND HISSES

Plan B. The next day in the Student Center.

Jennifer brought her own camera. And I brought a huge bag of Nutty Nutty candy bars.

Everyone loves Nutty Nutty Bars. You know their slogan: *They're So Nutty, They Make You Nutty, Too!*

The good thing about a Nutty Nutty Bar is that it sticks to your teeth. *No way* you can pull it off. So you have that great Nutty Nutty taste for *days!*

Normally I sell the Nutty Nutty Bars for two dollars each. But today was Plan B. Today everyone would see how popular I am. Mainly because I planned to give the candy bars away for *free*.

I met Jennifer after dinner in front of the game room. The Student Center was packed. Lots of kids hang out here every night. It's more fun than doing your homework.

"Get your camera ready," I told The Ecch. "When I start giving these babies away, I'll have a huge crowd around me. I'll be the most popular dude in the *universe*!"

I dragged my bag of candy into the game room. "Free candy bars!" I shouted. I raised a handful of candy bars over my head. "Come and get 'em! It's my birthday. And I'm giving out gifts! Free Nutty Nuttys!"

Can you *imagine* the excited cries and shouts? Bernie B. *giving something away?*

It looked like a cattle stampede. I was mobbed. All I could see were hands—hands grabbing the candy bars as fast as I pulled them from the bag.

"Jennifer—are you getting this?" I cried. "Are you getting their happy faces?"

I looked up to see her clicking away.

"Feenman, nice try," I said. "Beat it. You already grabbed four bars. Did you think I wasn't counting?"

Feenman grinned. He had Nutty Nutty nougat and nuts stuck to his teeth and both cheeks. His school blazer pocket was stuffed with candy bars.

"Free Nutty Nuttys!" I shouted to the crowd. "It's my birthday gift to everybody!"

Kids cheered and slapped me on the back as I handed out the candy. I turned to Jennifer. "Are you getting the looks on their faces? Do I look popular or what?"

"Yeaa, Bernie! Yeaa, Bernie!" kids started to chant.

"Yo, Chipmunk!" I called. "Come here, Chipper. Here's a candy bar!"

Chipmunk is the shyest guy in school. He's so shy, he burps into his shirt pocket so his breath won't go on anyone. When he enters a room, he says, "Goodbye"—just in case you don't want to talk to him.

"Chipper—catch!" I tossed him a Nutty Nutty. I knew he was too shy to come over and get it.

I turned to The Ecch. "Take a picture. Quick. Chipmunk enjoying his free candy bar—thanks to the most popular dude in school!"

Everyone cheered. Jennifer clicked away. Plan B was a big success.

But then I saw Chipmunk's face get weird. His eyes bulged. His mouth dropped open.

"HUNNNNH! HUNNNNNH!"

He started waving his arms wildly and making a horrible sound.

"HUNNNNNNH!"

"He's choking!" Feenman cried. "He's choking on the candy bar!"

I turned to Jennifer. "Stop taking his picture!"

"HUNNNNNH!"

Chipmunk's eyes bulged out of his head. His face turned bright purple. He was beating his chest with his fists.

At that moment Leif Blower walked in, followed by Mr. Pupipantz. They both stopped when they saw Chipmunk choking—and gasped.

"HUNNNNNNH!"

Leif tried to help Chipmunk. He gave him a slap on the back. Chipmunk heaved hard—and a big, wet glob of Nutty Nutty Bar came flying out of his mouth. It sailed across the room and hit Mr. Pupipantz in the forehead—and stuck there.

Chipmunk was bent over, panting hard. His face started to return to its normal color.

Mr. Pupipantz struggled to pull the candy bar glob off his forehead.

"What's going on here?" he cried. He squinted at Chipmunk. "Who gave you that candy bar?"

Chipmunk pointed. "Bernie did. He made me eat it so

he could take a picture. I—I guess he forgot I'm allergic to nuts. The nuts made my throat close, and I started to choke."

"Wait—I can explain!" I cried.

Everyone was staring at me. Kids started to boo and hiss. Some kids flung their candy bars back at me.

"Wait! Listen!" I cried. "OWWW!" A Nutty Nutty Bar hit me in the stomach. Candy bars bounced off my back.

"BOOOOOOOO!"

"HISSSSSSSS!"

"Jennifer—stop taking pictures!" I shouted. "Stop!"

She lowered her camera—and ducked as a bunch of Nutty Nutty Bars came sailing at me.

"BOOOOOOOO, BERNIE!" kids shouted angrily.

Jennifer turned her one blue eye and one brown eye on me. "Bernie," she said, "is it time for Plan C?"

Chapter 15

A NATURAL SWING

Birthday fever!

I could sense it. The whole Rotten School campus was buzzing about my birthday party.

NOT!

No one was talking about it. No one was making any big plans. And I *didn't have* a Plan C.

Wednesday afternoon, I ran into April-May June. She was carrying a tennis racket and heading toward the tennis courts across from R.U. Dumm Field.

I stepped in front of her to keep her from running

away. She's always so shy around me.

"Going to play tennis?" I asked.

"No. Just swatting flies," she said. She swung the racket hard.

I jumped back. "Missed me!" I cried. "You have an awesome backhand. A natural swing."

"Thanks, Bernie," she said. "The answer is no."

"But I didn't ask you anything," I said.

"Just in case," she said. She swung the racket again. This time she clipped the side of my face.

"No problem," I said, staggering around on the grass. "I'll put ice on it. It won't swell up much."

"Sorry," she said. "I wasn't aiming for your face. It just slipped a little."

I shook off the pain. "I know you've heard about my birthday party," I said. "Just give me a hint. What kind of birthday present are the girls cooking up for me?"

"I know what *I'm* giving you," April-May said.

I started to pant. My heart popped out of my chest. I had to push it back in.

"Really? What are you getting me?" I breathed.

"A picture of me," April-May said. "The picture

that will be on my page in the yearbook as Most Popular Rotten Egg."

I tossed back my head and laughed. I love a girl with a sharp sense of humor.

While I had my head tossed back, she flung her chewing gum into my open mouth.

"Bernie, are you really having a birthday party?" she asked.

I gulped down the gum. "Yeah, really," I said. "It's going to be the biggest party in the history of birthdays."

She squinted at me. "Then how come no one has heard about it?"

I swallowed. "Because it's a *surprise* party?" I uttered weakly.

She swung her racket again. This time it just brushed my hair back. I watched her run across the grass toward the tennis courts.

I had a heavy feeling—like a bowling ball—in the pit of my stomach. The party wasn't happening. Was it time to panic?

I couldn't let Sherman Oaks or April-May June win that yearbook page. I knew I was Most Popular.

But how could I prove it to Blower if the biggest party in birthday party history never happened?

And then ... more bad news.

Belzer came running across the grass. "Bernie, Headmaster Upchuck wants to see you. Right away."

Chapter 16

A REMINDER FROM THE UPCHUCK

"Did he have a smile on his face?" I asked Belzer. "I'll bet he wants to give me the Good Citizen Award for this month."

"I don't think he was smiling," Belzer said.

I started to shake. Uh-oh. He wasn't calling me in for doughnuts and chocolate milk.

What did I do wrong this week? I could only count twenty or thirty things.

I put a big grin on my face as I stepped into the Headmaster's office. He's so short, I had to stand on tiptoe and lean over his desk to see him.

"Nice to see you, sir," I said. "I love that new tie. What are those colored streaks supposed to be? Is it modern art?"

He glanced down at the tie. "It's not modern art, Bernie," he growled. "I spilled some of my Froot Loops on it at breakfast."

"Well, it looks wonderful on you," I said. "Why did you call me in, sir? Do you need some help with the first graders? You know I'm always eager to volunteer."

"I have chapped lips. Don't make me laugh," The Upchuck said. "I called you in to give you a short message."

I flashed him my two-dimpled smile. "And what is that message, sir? If it has to do with the five missing pepperoni pizzas from the kitchen, I can explain that."

His bald head turned red. He lowered himself from his chair and pulled himself up to his full, three-foot height. "Here's my message for you, Bernie," he said. "It's just a little reminder."

"Reminder, sir?"

He nodded. "Whatever it is you're doing? Don't do it!"

He climbed back into his chair.

"Is that it, sir?" I asked.

"That's it," he said.

"Thank you, sir," I said. I gave him a two-finger salute.

I turned and walked into his outer office. I let out a sigh of relief. I got off pretty easy that time.

I really *couldn't* explain about the five missing pepperoni pizzas. We guys got hungry late one night, that's all.

I headed for the door, then stopped. Someone was bent behind the long desk, shoving files into a bottom drawer. When he stood up, I recognized him.

Angel Goodeboy.

"Hey," he called. "Bernie, what's up?"

Angel looks like an angel. He has a pink-cheeked round face, innocent blue eyes, a tiny red mouth, and a pile of blond, curly hair. I always picture him with a silver halo floating over his head.

The girls all adore him. Guys think he's the sweetest dude in school. But I know the truth about him.

Angel is no angel.

"What are you doing here in The Upchuck's office?" I asked him. "I mean, what are you being punished for?"

He giggled. "Me? Punished? No way, Bernie. I'm working here. You know. Filing stuff. And looking up records and stuff on the computer."

"Do you get paid?" I asked.

He shook his head. "No. I'm doing it just for the fun."

What a weirdo!

Then he leaned over the desk and whispered, "Bernie, I heard about your birthday party. I'm totally excited about it."

I blinked. "You are?"

"Let me help out," he said. "Please?"

I blinked again. Was I dreaming this? Angel and I weren't exactly best buddies.

"Help out? How?" I asked.

His blue eyes twinkled. "Well...I can get all the girls to come. They think I'm adorable. And I can get my Nyce House friends. And guess what, Bernie? My brothers and sisters are coming for a visit. They'll come, too."

"You're serious?" I said. This could be good. I knew that Angel had a *lot* of brothers and sisters!

"My brother Angel is coming," Angel said.

"He's named Angel, too?" I asked.

He grinned. "Yes, he's Angel the third. My brother Happy Goodeboy is coming. And Gladdy Goodeboy and Goody Goodeboy and my sister Beeya Goodeboy and my cousin Attsa Goodeboy."

"Guess we'll have a good crowd," I said.

"Let me take care of everything," Angel begged. "Please, Bernie. Put me in charge. I want the party to be a real surprise for you."

I squinted at him. I knew I couldn't trust him. Was he for real?

I studied his face. I stared into his eyes. I pinched his cheek really hard. I pulled out his tongue and examined it carefully.

Yes. He was for real. I wasn't dreaming this.

"You really think I should trust you?" I said. "You really want this party to be a success?"

"Give me a chance," he said. "I'll work so hard! I'll talk it up so much, I'll have blisters in my mouth! I promise."

"You promise?"

He flashed me his angelic grin. I could see the silver halo bobbing above his curly, blond hair.

Should I trust him?

Should I?

I was desperate. I wanted to believe him. "Okay. You're on," I said.

"I promise it'll be the biggest surprise party in the history of Rotten School!" he said.

And guess what?

He wasn't lying....

Chapter 17

TIME TO PARTY

Party Day!

I did a happy tap dance in front of the mirror. My heart was tap dancing, too.

I could feel the excitement. Feel the LOVE!

I knew the party had to be HUGE. All week I saw Angel running around the campus, talking to every kid in school. He went to all three dorms. He grabbed kids after school in the Student Center and in the gym. I saw him running after the soccer team on the R.U. Dumm Field in the rain.

Who could resist him?

Angel put up signs in front of every building. They showed a big birthday cake with a million candles, and they read:

PARTY OF THE CENTURY!
IF YOU MISS IT, YOU'LL MISS IT!

I liked the sign a lot. But Angel left out one important thing. I scurried around with a black marker, and on the bottom of each one, I wrote: BRING PRESENTS!!!

Now the big day had finally arrived. I stood in front of my mirror and practiced acting surprised.

"A party for me? You shouldn't have!"

"All those presents? They CAN'T be for *me!*"

"Wow! I'm totally surprised! Awesome! What a surprise!"

I practiced gasping in shock. And I practiced the wish I'd make over my birthday candles: *Please make me Most Popular Rotten Egg.*

"Okay, Big B," I told myself in the mirror. "It's showtime! Let's go to the party and be surprised!"

My heart was still tap dancing. My brain was zipping and zapping. My whole body tingled like electricity as I walked to the Student Center.

I took a deep breath, put on my best smile, and stepped into the party.

And guess what, dudes and dudettes?

I really WAS surprised!

My eyes goggled. My mouth dropped open.

And I let out a SCREAM OF HORROR!

Chapter 18

SURPRISE!!!

My scream echoed off the tile walls. It finally faded
to a whimper, and I dropped to my knees. My whole
body quivered and shook. My tongue rolled down to
the floor.

Why was I gripped with a trembling horror?

Well, as I stepped into the party room, the first
thing I saw were the big red and yellow banners on
the walls:

HAPPY BIRTHDAY, ANGEL!

Then I saw cutouts of angels with bright halos
dangling on strings from the ceiling. Angels on the

walls. Angels everywhere.

Kids poured into the room. They lined up to hand Angel birthday gifts. On a table in a corner I saw a huge white birthday cake shaped like Angel's head.

Angel was grinning and slapping high fives and piling up the gifts. When he saw me, he came trotting over. "SURPRISE!" he yelled.

He took me by the arm and pulled me up from the floor. He rolled my tongue back into my mouth. "Welcome to my party, Bernie!" he said.

"Y-y-y-y-" My mouth wouldn't work. My legs wobbled. My eyes rolled around in my head like marbles.

"What's up with *this?*" I finally managed to cry. I pointed to the banners, the angels, the cake. "Happy Birthday, *ANGEL?* How did this get to be YOUR party?"

His blue eyes flashed. "Bernie," he said, "remember, I work in Headmaster Upchuck's office?"

"I remember," I said.

"Well, I got out the school directory," Angel said. "And I called your parents. I wanted to invite them to your birthday party. But you know what they told me?"

"Wh-what?" I stammered.

"They told me your birthday isn't for ANOTHER FOUR MONTHS!"

Busted!

The dude caught me!

Think fast, Bernie. Think fast....

"So? I like to start celebrating *early!*" I said.

Angel patted me on the back. "Don't feel bad. But I just didn't think it was fair."

"F-fair?" I muttered weakly. "F-fair?"

"Today is my real birthday," Angel said. "That's why the party is for ME!"

"But—but—"

"Catch you later, Bernie," Angel said. "I have to pass out the I ♥ ANGEL T-shirts—and collect more presents! Do you believe how POPULAR I am? I must be the most popular kid in school!"

He winked at me. "I hope Leif Blower is watching!" Then he ran off to greet more kids.

Chapter 19

GOT CAKE?

No! No! No!

Angels stared down at me from the walls, from the ceiling. I had to shut my eyes.

HAPPY BIRTHDAY, ANGEL?!

All of my planning. All of my plotting...

HAPPY BIRTHDAY, ANGEL?!

Feenman and Crench shuffled over to me. They were both shoving big slices of pizza into their mouths. They had gobs of cheese dripping down their chins.

"*Mmmmph.* Awesome party," Feenman said.

"The best!" Crench said. "You *glmmmmph mum-mmph* having a good time, Bernie?"

A good time?

Does a roast turkey have a good time at Thanksgiving?

Well, I was the turkey at *this* party!

That dirty double-crosser Angel ruined everything for me.

Now what could I do?

"Time to light the candles!" Angel shouted. "Come on, everyone. I'm going to make a wish. I'm going to wish for world peace!"

Everyone gathered around the cake. I dropped down at a table and buried my head in my hands.

I heard heavy footsteps behind me. I turned and saw Jennifer Ecch lumber into the room. I couldn't really see her face. She was carrying an enormous birthday cake in front of her.

She stopped when she heard everyone singing "Happy Birthday" to Angel. She peered around the side of her cake—and saw Angel's fluffy, white cake, candles glowing.

I saw her mouth drop open in surprise. The huge

cake almost fell from her hands. She lurched over to my table. "Bernie—what's up with this? Am I in the wrong room?"

"There's been a little change," I said. "It's a birthday party for Angel."

"But—but—" she sputtered. "I spent five days baking this cake! Each layer is a different flavor! Why didn't you tell me the party was changed?"

"Jennifer, I'm sorry," I said. "I didn't know. I—"

"I stayed up three nights in a row writing WUBBY-WUBBY all over it in pink icing!" Jennifer boomed. "I flunked two tests because of all the time I spent working on your cake. And it was all for nothing? All for *nothing?*"

"Don't get excited," I said. "We can think of something to do with it!"

"But—but—but—" she sputtered.

April-May came running over. She had a strange smile on her face. "Jennifer, let me handle this," she said. "I just thought of something we can do with the cake."

"Well . . . okay," Jennifer said. She handed the cake to April-May.

And April-May dumped it over my head.

The heavy, wet cake and the thick, yellow icing with WUBBY-WUBBY all over it glopped down my face, oozed over my shoulders, and rolled down my entire body.

I sat there for a long while.

Finally I needed to breathe. Using both hands, I scooped cake and icing away from my nose, then my eyes.

I blinked several times. Wiped thick gobs of cake from my shoulders. Blinked some more. April-May and Jennifer were slapping high fives and touching knuckles and pumping their fists in the air in victory.

"Bernie, you're not having a great day," I told myself. I wiped away another glob of icing—and realized my bad day wasn't over.

Leif Blower had just entered the room.

Chapter 20

AND THE WINNER IS . . .

With a groan, I watched Leif Blower walk over to the group of kids around Angel's birthday cake. April-May June clung to one of Leif's arms. Sherman Oaks walked at his other side, stuffing hundred-dollar bills into Leif's shirt pocket.

I couldn't *stand* it. I couldn't stand to lose the Most Popular Rotten Egg page this way.

Think fast, Bernie ... Think fast ...

Slipping and sliding in yellow icing, I slumped over to Blower. Clumps of yellow cake hit the floor with every step I took.

"Pretty good little party," I said. "If I say so myself. Angel was so surprised that I threw this big party for him!"

Blower squinted at me. "*You* threw this party for Angel?"

I nodded. "Yes, a surprise party was all my idea. I like to do nice things for people. That's why I'm so popular. I spent days and days planning this party. But it was worth it just to see all my friends' happy faces!"

April-May stared at me. "Bernie, why are you covered in cake?"

I shrugged. "I like cake."

Blower stuck a finger into the icing on my chest, pulled off a gob, and tasted it. "Not bad."

"Have fun at my party, guys," I said. "I didn't do it to make myself popular. I did it all for my friend Angel."

Blower took another glob of icing off my chest. "I'm totally impressed!" he said. "You did an awesome job, Bernie. Every kid in school came to this party.

It's the biggest birthday party in school history!"

I swallowed hard. "So . . . does that mean that you're gonna pick Angel or me to be Most Popular Rotten Egg?"

"No way," Blower said. April-May squeezed his hand. Sherman giggled.

My heart jumped. "Then who are you going to choose?" I asked.

A grin spread over Blower's face. "You know, Bernie, because of the Most Popular Rotten Egg yearbook page, kids have been giving ME presents. And inviting ME to parties. And hanging on to MY arm."

April-May tightened her grip on his arm.

"It made me realize," Blower said, "that I'M the most popular kid at Rotten School. So I put MYSELF on that page!"

"Gaaaaack."

A hideous *gaaaack* escaped my throat. I just couldn't hold it in.

"Gaaaaaack."

I *gaaaaacked* again.

April-May and Sherman applauded. "Good choice, Leif!" they cried.

Blower stuck out his hand. "Congratulate me, Bernie. I've named *myself* Most Popular Rotten Egg!"

"*Gaaaaaack.* You definitely are a Rotten Egg!" I replied.

I pulled a *Wubby-Wubby* off my forehead and started to eat it. "Mmmmmm. Not bad."

HERE'S A SNEAK PEEK AT BOOK #14

R.L. STINE'S

THE BEAST
FROM PRESCHOOL

Yes, life can be scary these days at Rotten School.

Why were kids terrifying one another every night? Well, I promised I'd explain.

It all started on Welcome Back Day.

That's a tradition started many years ago by our school's founder, Mr. I. B. Rotten. Every year Headmaster Upchuck welcomes back some dude or dudette who graduated from our school.

The person gives a speech to the whole school. You know. To inspire us. To tell us how being in Rotten School prepares us to go out into the world and do great things.

I remember the speaker from Welcome Back Day last year. It was a woman who had a knitting needle stuck in her nose. She talked about how you can still have an awesome life, even with a knitting needle in your nose.

Two years ago the speaker was the guy who invented diapers for horses.

We have a *lot* of cool graduates from our school.

But *this* year's visitor was the coolest of all, even cooler than the horse diaper guy. And we were totally crazed and excited because...

... this year's speaker was our favorite horror movie director, Mr. B. A. Gool.

As we all piled into the auditorium, my buddies and I argued over which was Gool's creepiest film.

"It's gotta be *The Beast from Preschool!*" Crench said. "Remember that dude? He was only four years old, but he could bite your throat out."

My buddy Belzer gave Crench a shove. "That wasn't scary at all," he said. "Know which one totally freaked me out? *I'll Eat Your Face for Breakfast*. After that movie, I couldn't eat breakfast for a *month!*"

"Too babyish," Crench said. "My two-year-old sister liked that one. Gool's scariest film has to be *My Hair Is Alive!* I couldn't sleep for six weeks. I worried if I went to sleep, my hair would strangle me."

They turned to me. "What do you think, Big B?" Belzer asked.

Before I could answer, Sherman Oaks bumped up between us. He tossed back his blond hair and flashed us his perfect, sixty-five-toothed smile.

"Anyone got change for a hundred?" he asked. He waved a hundred-dollar bill in my face. "Or can anyone change this *five*-hundred-dollar bill?" He waved it under my nose.

Sherman does that every day. He doesn't want change. He just likes to make me drool.

He is the richest kid at Rotten School. He's so rich, he pays a kid to burp for him.

"Dudes, check this out," he said. He stuck out his left sneaker.

I saw a small silver screen on top of the sneaker. "What's that for?" I asked. "A viewer so you can see what you're stepping into?"

"The sneaker is a DVD player," Sherman said. "I downloaded twenty-eight B. A. Gool movies onto it. I watch them on my shoe while I walk to class."

Sherman raised the shoe higher. "See? The volume control is on the toe part," he said. "The shoe cost five thousand dollars. My parents sent it to me cuz they think they can buy my love."

"Cool," I said. "What does the other sneaker do?"

"It's an MP3 player," Sherman said. "I downloaded two thousand songs onto it."

We jammed into the auditorium and found seats near the front. Headmaster Upchuck was already on the stage. He's only about three feet tall. He's so short, he has to stand on a ladder to look in the mirror to comb his hair!

The Headmaster stood on a tall stool, trying to reach the microphone.

I could tell Belzer was excited. He kept kicking the seat in front of him. "What do you think B. A. Gool looks like?" he asked. "He's *got* to be way weird, right?"

"He probably wears a long, black cape," Crench said.

"Maybe he has fangs," Feenman said. "And really pale white skin . . . because he has no blood. And they'll have to keep the auditorium lights off because bright light will melt him."

"I'll bet he's like some kinda monster," Belzer said. "He's got to be way weird to make movies like those."

Up on the stage, Headmaster Upchuck tapped the microphone. "Welcome back to Welcome Back Day," he said. "I want to welcome back everyone to our Welcome Back celebration."

His stool tilted. He started to fall off.

Everyone cheered.

But he caught himself by grabbing on to the microphone.

Everyone groaned.

"And now," he said, "let's welcome back to Welcome Back Day one of our most famous graduates. Let's give a real Rotten welcome to . . . B. A. Gool!"

We all cheered and jumped up and down and went nuts.

And there he came, B. A. Gool, walking onto the stage . . . and everyone *gasped in shock!*

ABOUT THE AUTHOR

photo by Dan Nelken

R.L. Stine graduated from Rotten School with a solid D+ average, which put him at the top of his class. He says that his favorite activities at school were Scratching Body Parts and Making Armpit Noises.

In sixth grade, R.L. won the school Athletic Award for his performance in the Wedgie Championships. Unfortunately, after the tournament, his underpants had to be surgically removed.

R.L. was very popular in school. He could tell this because kids always clapped and cheered whenever he left the room. One of his teachers remembers him fondly: "R.L. was a hard worker. He was so proud of himself when he learned to wave bye-bye with both hands."

After graduation, R.L. became well known for writing scary book series such as The Nightmare Room, Fear Street, Goosebumps, and Mostly Ghostly, and a short story collection called *Beware!*

Today, R.L. lives in a cage in New York City, where he is busy writing stories about his school days. Says he: "I wish everyone could be a Rotten Student."

For more information
about R.L. Stine,
go to www.rottenschool.com
and www.rlstine.com